The Watter's Mou'

CH01003477

Books by Bram Stoker

Novels
- *Crooken Sands*
- *Dracula*
- *Lady Athlyne*
- *Miss Betty*
- *The Jewel of Seven Stars*
- *The Lady of the Shroud*
- *The Lair of the White Worm* (originally published in the United States as *The Garden of Evil*)
- *The Man from Shorrox's*
- *The Man* (also published as *The Gates of Life*)
- *The Mystery of the Sea*
- *The Shoulder of Shasta*
- *The Snake's Pass*
- *The Watter's Mou*

Collections
- *Dracula's Guest*
- *Snowbound*
- *Under the Sunset*

Nonfiction
- *Sir Henry Irving and Miss Ellen Terry*
- *A Glimpse of America*
- *Famous Impostors*
- *Personal Reminiscences of Henry Irving*
- *The Duties of Clerks of Petty Sessions in Ireland*

The Watter's Mou'

BRAM STOKER

WILDSIDE PRESS
Doylestown, Pennsylvania

The Watter's Mou'
A publication of
Wildside Press
P.O. Box 301
Holicong, PA 18928-0301

www.wildsidepress.com

I

*I*t threatened to be a wild night. All day banks of sea fog had come and gone, sweeping on shore with the southeast wind, which is so fatal at Cruden Bay, and indeed all along the coast of Aberdeenshire, and losing themselves in the breezy expanses of the high uplands beyond. As yet the wind only came in puffs, followed by intervals of ominous calm; but the barometer had been falling for days, and the sky had on the previous night been streaked with great "mare's-tails" running in the direction of the dangerous wind. Up to early morning the wind had been southwesterly, but had then "backed" to southeast; and the sudden change, no less than the backing, was ominous indeed. From the waste of sea came a ceaseless muffled roar, which seemed loudest and most full of dangerous import when it came through the mystery of the driving fog. Whenever the fog-belts would lift or disperse, or disappear inland before the gusts of wind, the sea

would look as though swept with growing anger; for
though there were neither big waves as during a storm,
nor a great swell as after one, all the surface of the water
as far as the eye could reach was covered with little
waves tipped with white. Closer together grew these
waves as the day wore on, the angrier ever the curl of
the white water where they broke. In the North Sea it
does not take long for the waves to rise; and all along
the eastern edge of Buchan it was taken for granted
that there would be wild work on the coast before the
night was over.

In the little look-out house on the top of the cliff
over the tiny harbor of Port Erroll the coastguard on
duty was pacing rapidly to and fro. Every now and
again he would pause, and lifting a field-glass from the
desk, sweep the horizon from Girdleness at the south
of Aberdeen, when the lifting of the mist would let
him see beyond the Scaurs, away to the north, where
the high cranes of the Blackman quarries at Murdoch
Head seemed to cleave the sky like gigantic gallows
trees.

He was manifestly in high spirits, and from the
manner in which, one after another, he looked again
and again at the Martini-Henry rifle in the rack, the
navy revolver stuck muzzle down on a spike, and the
cutlass in its sheath hanging on the wall, it was easy to
see that his interest arose from something connected
with his work as a coastguard. On the desk lay an open
telegram smoothed down by his hard hands, with the
brown envelope lying beside it. It gave some sort of
clue to his excitement, although it did not go into
detail. "Keep careful watch tonight; run expected; spare
no efforts; most important."

William Barrow, popularly known as Sailor Willy,
was a very young man to be a chief boatman in the

preventive service, albeit that his station was one of the smallest on the coast. He had been allowed, as a reward for saving the life of his lieutenant, to join the coast service, and had been promoted to chief boatman as a further reward for a clever capture of smugglers, wherein he had shown not only great bravery, but much ability and power of rapid organization.

The Aberdeen coast is an important one in the way of guarding on account of the vast number of fishing-smacks which, during the season, work from Peterhead up and down the coast, and away on the North Sea right to the shores of Germany and Holland. This vast coming and going affords endless opportunities for smuggling; and, despite of all vigilance, a considerable amount of "stuff" finds its way to the consumers without the formality of the Custom House. The fish traffic is a quick traffic, and its returns come all at once, so that a truly enormous staff would be requisite to examine adequately the thousand fish-smacks that use the harbor of Peterhead, and on Sundays pack its basins with a solid mass of boats. The coastline for some forty miles south is favorable for this illicit traffic. The gneiss and granite formations broken up by every convulsion of nature, and worn by the strain and toil of ages into every conceivable form of rocky beauty, offers an endless variety of narrow creeks and bays where the daring, to whom the rocks and the currents and the tides are known, may find secret entrance and speedy exit for their craft. This season the smuggling had been chiefly of an overt kind — that is, the goods had been brought into the harbor amongst the fish and nets, and had been taken through the streets under the eyes of the unsuspecting Customs officers. Some of these takes were so large, that the authorities had made up their minds that there must be a great amount of smuggling going on. The secret agents in the German, Dutch, Flemish, and French ports were asked to make extra exertions in discovering the amount of the illicit trade, and their later reports were of an almost alarming nature. They said that really vast amounts of tobacco, brandy, rum, silks, laces, and all sorts of excisable commodities were being secretly shipped in the British fishing-fleet; and as only a very small proportion of this was discovered, it was manifest that smuggling to a large extent was once more to the fore. Accordingly precautions were doubled all along the east coast frequented by the fishing-fleets. Not only were the coastguards warned of the danger and cautioned against devices which might keep them from their work at critical times, but they were apprised of every new shipment as reported from abroad. Furthermore, the detectives of the service were sent about to parts where the men were suspected of laxity — or worse.

Thus it was that Sailor Willy, with the experience of two promotions for cause, and with the sense of responsibility that belonged to his office, felt in every way elated at the possibility of some daring work before him. He knew, of course, that a similar telegram had been received at every station on the coast, and that the chance of an attempt being made in Cruden Bay or its surroundings was a small one; but he was young and brave and hopeful, and with an adamantine sense of integrity to support him in his work. It was unfortunate that his comrade was absent, ill in the hospital at Aberdeen, and that the strain at present on the service, together with the men away on annual training and in the naval maneuvers, did not permit of a substitute being sent to him. However, he felt strong enough to undertake any amount of duty — he was strong enough and handsome enough to have a good opinion of himself, and too brave and too sensible to let his head be turned by vanity.

As he walked to and fro there was in the distance of his mind — in that dim background against which in a man's mind a woman's form finds suitable projection — some sort of vague hope that a wild dream of rising in the world might be some time realized. He knew that every precaution in his power had been already taken, and felt that he could indulge in fancies without detriment to his work. He had signaled the coastguard at Whinnyfold on the south side of the Bay, and they had exchanged ideas by means of the signal language. His appliances for further signaling by day or night were in perfect order, and he had been right over his whole boundary since he had received the telegram seeing that all things were in order. Willy Barrow was not one to leave things to chance where duty was concerned.

His daydreams were not all selfish. They were at least so far unselfish that the results were to be shared with another; for Willy Barrow was engaged to be married. Maggie MacWhirter was the daughter of an old fisherman who had seen days more prosperous than the present. He had once on a time owned a fishing-smack, but by degrees he had been compelled to borrow on her, till now, when, although he was nominal owner, the boat was so heavily mortgaged that at any moment he might lose his entire possession. That such an event was not unlikely was manifest, for the mortgagee was no other than Solomon Mendoza of Hamburg and Aberdeen, who had changed in like manner the ownership of a hundred boats, and who had the reputation of being as remorseless as he was rich. MacWhirter had long been a widower, and Maggie since a little girl had kept house for her father and her two brothers, Andrew and Niel. Andrew was twenty-seven — six years older than Maggie — and Niel had just turned twenty. The elder brother was a quiet, self-contained, hard-working man, who now and again manifested great determination, though generally at unexpected times; the younger was rash, impetuous, and passionate, and though in his moments of quiescence more tender to those he cared for than was usual with men of his class, he was a never-ending source of anxiety to his father and his sister. Andrew, or Sandy as he was always called, took him with consistent quietness.

The present year, although a good one in the main, had been but poor for MacWhirter's boat. Never once had he had a good take of fish — not one-half the number of crans of the best boat; and the season was so far advanced, and the supply had been so plentiful, that a few days before, the notice had been up at Peterhead that after the following week the buyers would not take any more herring.

This notice naturally caused much excitement, and the whole fishing industry determined to make every effort to improve the shining hours left to them. Exertions were on all sides redoubled, and on sea and shore there was little idleness. Naturally the smuggling interest bestirred itself too; its chance for the year was in the rush and bustle and hurry of the coming and going fleet, and anything held over for a chance had to be ventured now or left over for a year — which might mean indefinitely. Great ventures were therefore taken by some of the boats; and from their daring the authorities concluded that either heavy bribes were given, or else that the goods were provided by others than the fishermen who undertook to run them. A few important seizures, however, made the men wary; and it was understood from the less frequent but greater importance of the seizures, that the price for "running" had greatly gone up. There was much passionate excitement amongst those who were found out and their friends, and a general wish to discover the informers. Some of the smuggling fishermen at first refused to pay the fines until they were told who had informed. This position being unsupportable, they had instead paid the fines and cherished hatred in their hearts. Some of the more reckless and turbulent spirits had declared their intention of avenging themselves on the informers when they should be known. It was only natural that this feeling of rage should extend to the Customs officers and men of the preventive service, who stood between the unscrupulous adventurers and their harvest; and altogether matters had become somewhat strained between the fishermen and the authorities.

The Port Erroll boats, like those from Collieston, were all up at Peterhead, and of course amongst them MacWhirter's boat the Sea Gull with her skipper and his two sons. It was now Friday night, and the boats had been out for several days, so that it was pretty certain that there would be a full harbor at Peterhead on the Saturday. A marriage had been arranged to take place this evening between Thomas Keith of Boddam and Alice MacDonald, whose father kept the public house The Jamie Fleeman on the northern edge of the Erroll estate. Though the occasion was to be a grand one, the notice of it had been short indeed. It was said by the bride's friends that it had been fixed so hurriedly because the notice of the closing of the fishing season had been so suddenly given out at Peterhead. Truth to tell, some sort of explanation was necessary, for it was only on Wednesday morning that word had been sent to the guests, and as these came from all sorts of places between Peterhead and Collieston, and taking a sweep of some ten miles inland, there was need of some preparation. The affair was to top all that had ever been seen at Port Erroll, and as The Jamie Fleeman was but a tiny place — nothing, in fact, but a wayside public-house — it was arranged that it was to take place in the new barn and storehouses Matthew Beagrie had just built on the inner side of the sand hills, where they came close to the Water of Cruden.

Throughout all the east side of Buchan there had for some time existed a wonder amongst the quiet-going people as to the strange prosperity of MacDonald. His public-house had, of course, a practical monopoly; for as there was not a licensed house on the Erroll estate, and as his was the nearest house of call to the port, he naturally got what custom there was going. The fishermen all along the coast for some seven or eight miles went to him either to drink or to get their liquor for drinking elsewhere; and not a few of the Collieston men on their Saturday journey home from Peterhead and their Sunday journey out there again made a detour to have a glass and a chat and a pipe, if time permitted, with "Tammas Mac" — for such was his sobriquet. To the authorities he and his house were also sources of interest; for there was some kind of suspicion that some of the excellent brandy and cigars that he dispensed had arrived by a simpler road than that through the Custom House. It was at this house, in the good old days of smuggling that the coastguards used to be entertained when a run was on foot, and where they slept off their drunkenness whilst the cargoes were being hidden or taken inland in the ready carts. Of course all this state of things had been altered, and there was as improved a decorum amongst the smugglers, as there was a sterner rule and discipline amongst the coastguards. It was many a long year since Philip Kennedy met his death at Kirkton at the hands of the exciseman Anderson. Comparatively innocent deception was now the smugglers' only wile.

Tonight the whole countryside was to be at the wedding, and the dance that was to follow it; and for this occasion the lion was to lie down with the lamb, for the coastguards were bidden to the feast with the rest. Sailor Willy had looked forward to the dance with delight, for Maggie was to be there, and on the Billy Ruffian, which had been his last ship, he had been looked on as the best dancer before the mast. If there be any man who shuns a dance in which he knows he can shine, and at which his own particular girl is to be present, that man is not to be found in the Royal Naval Marine, even amongst those of them who have joined in the preventive service. Maggie was no less delighted, although she had a source of grief which for the present she had kept all to herself. Her father had of late been much disturbed about affairs. He had not spoken of them to her, and she did not dare to mention the matter to him; for old MacWhirter was a closemouthed man, and did not exchange many confidences even with his own children. But Maggie guessed at the cause of the sadness — of the down-bent head when none were looking; the sleepless nights and the deep smothered groans that now and again marked his heavy sleep told the tale loudly enough to reach the daughter's ears. For the last few weeks, whenever her father was at home, Maggie had herself lain awake listening, listening, in increasing agony of spirit, for one of these half moans or for the sound of the tossing of the restless man. He was as gentle and kind to his daughter as ever; but on his leaving the last time there had been an omission on his part that troubled her to the quick. For the first time in his life he had not kissed her as he went away.

On the previous day Sailor Willy had said he would come to the wedding and the dance if his duties should permit him; and, when asked if he could spare a few rockets for the occasion, promised that he would let off three Board of Trade rockets, which he could now deal with as it was three months since he had used any. He was delighted at the opportunity of meeting the fisherfolk and his neighbors; for his officers had impressed on him the need of being on good terms with all around him, both for the possibility which it would always afford him of knowing how things were going on, and for the benefit of the rocket-service whenever there might be need of willing hands and hearts to work with him, for in the Board of Trade rocket-service much depends on voluntary aid. That very afternoon he had fixed the rockets on the wall of the barn with staples, so that he could fire them from below with a slow match, which he fixed ready. When he had got the telegram he had called in to Maggie and told her if he did not come to fetch her she was to go on to the wedding by herself, and that he would try to join her later. She had appeared a little startled when he told her he might not be present; but after a pause smiled, and said she would go, and that he was not to lose any time coming when he was free. Now that every arrangement was complete, and as he had between puffs of the sea-fog got a clean sweep of the horizon and saw that there was no sail of any kind within sight, he thought he might have a look through the village and keep in evidence so as not to create any suspicion in the minds of the people. As he went through the street he noticed that nearly every house door was closed — all the women were at the new barn. It was now eight o'clock, and the darkness, which is slow of coming in the North, was closing in. Down by the barn there were quite a number of carts, and the horses had not been taken out, though the wedding was not to be till nine o'clock, or perhaps even later; for Mrs. MacDonald had taken care to tell her friends that Keith might not get over from Boddam till late. Willy looked at the carts carefully — some idea seemed to have struck him. Their lettering showed them to be from all parts round, and the names mostly of those who had not the best reputation. When his brief survey was finished he looked round and then went swiftly behind the barn so that no one might see him. As he went he muttered reflectively:

"Too many light carts and fast horses — too much silence in the barn — too little liquor going, to be all safe. There's something up here tonight." He was under the lee of the barn and looked up where he had fixed the rockets ready to fire. This gave him a new idea.

"I fixed them low so as to go over the sand hills and not be noticeable at Collieston or beyond. They are now placed up straight and will be seen for fifty miles if the weather be clear."

It was too dark to see very clearly, and he would not climb up to examine them lest he should be noticed and his purpose of acquiring information frustrated; but then and there he made up his mind that Port Erroll or its neighborhood had been the spot chosen for the running of the smuggled goods. He determined to find out more, and straightaway went round to the front and entered the room.

II

As soon as Sailor Willy was seen to enter, a large part of the gathering looked relieved, and at once began to chat and gabble in marked contrast to their previous gloom and silence. Port Erroll was well represented by its womankind, and by such of its men as were not away at the fishing; for it was the intention to mask the smuggling scheme by an assemblage at which all the respectability would be present. There appeared to be little rivalry between the two shoemakers, MacPherson and Beagrie, who chatted together in a corner, the former telling his companion how he had just been down to the lifeboathouse to see, as one of the Committee, that it was all ready in case it should be wanted before the night was over. Lang John and Lang Jim, the policemen of the place, looked sprucer even than usual, and their buttons shone in the light of the many paraffin lamps as if they had been newly burnished. Mitchell and his companions of the salmon fishery were grouped in another corner, and Andrew Mason was telling Mackay, the new flesher, whose shed was erected on the edge of the burn opposite John Reid's shop, of a great crab which he had taken that morning in a pot opposite the Twa Een.

But these and nearly all the other Port Erroll folk present were quiet, and their talk was of local interest; the main clack of tongues came from the many strange men who stood in groups near the center of the room and talked loudly. In the midst of them was the bridegroom, more joyous than any, though in the midst of his laughter he kept constantly turning to look at the door. The minister from Peterhead sat in a corner with the bride and her mother and father — the latter of whom, despite his constant laughter, had an anxious look on his face. Sailor Willy was greeted joyously, and the giver of the feast and the bridegroom each rose, and, taking a bottle and glass, offered him a drink.

"To the bride," said he; but seeing that no one else was drinking, he tapped the bridegroom on the shoulder, "Come, drink this with me, my lad!" he added. The latter paused an instant and then helped himself from MacDonald's bottle. Willy did not fail to notice the act, and holding out his glass said:

"Come, my lad, you drink with me! Change glasses in old style!" An odd pallor passed quickly across the bridegroom's face, but MacDonald spoke quickly:

"Tak it, mon, tak it!" So he took the glass, crying "No heel-taps," threw back his head, and raised the glass. Willy threw back his head too, and tossed off his liquor, but, as he did so, took care to keep a sharp eye on the other, and saw him, instead of swallowing his liquor, pour it into his thick beard. His mind was quite made up now. They meant to keep him out of the way by fair means or foul.

Just then two persons entered the room, one of them, James Cruickshank of the Kilmarnock Arms, who was showing the way to the other, an elderly man with a bald head, keen eyes, a ragged grey beard, a hooked nose, and an evil smile. As he entered MacDonald jumped up and came over to greet him.

"Oh! Mr. Mendoza, this is braw! We hopit tae see ye the nicht, but we were that feared that ye wadna come."

"Mein Gott, but why shall I not come — on this occasion of all — the occasion of the marriage of the daughter of mein goot frient, Tam Smack? And more-overs when I bring these as I haf promise. For you, mein frient Keith, this check, which one week you cash, and for you, my tear Miss Alice, these so bright neck-lace, which you will wear, ant which will sell if so you choose."

As he spoke he handed his gifts to the groom and bride. He then walked to the corner where Mrs. Mac sat, exchanging a keen look with his host as he did so. The latter seemed to have taken his cue and spoke out at once.

"And now, reverend sir, we may proceed — all is ready." As he spoke the bridal pair stood up, and the friends crowded round. Sailor Willy moved towards the door, and just as the parson opened his book, began to pass out. Tammas Mac immediately spoke to him:

"Ye're no gangin', Sailor Willy? Sure ye'll wait and see Tam Keith marrit on my lass?"

He instantly replied: "I must go for a while. I have some things to do, and then I want to try to bring Maggie down for the dance!" and before anything could be said, he was gone.

The instant he left the door he slipped round to the back of the barn, and running across the sand hills to

the left, crossed the wooden bridge, and hurrying up
the roadway by the cottage on the cliff gained the
watch-house. He knew that none of the company in
the barn could leave till the service was over, with the
minister's eye on them, without giving cause for after
suspicion; and he knew, too, that as there were no
windows on the south side of the barn, nothing could
be seen from that side. Without a moment's delay he
arranged his signals for the call for aid; and as the
rockets whizzed aloft, sending a white glare far into the
sky, he felt that the struggle had entered on its second
stage.

The night had now set in with a darkness unusual
in August. The swaithes of sea-mist whirled in by the
wind came fewer and fainter, and at times a sudden
rift through the driving clouds showed that there was
starlight somewhere between the driving masses of mist
and gloom. Willy Barrow once more tried all his weapons and saw that all his signals were in order. Then he
strapped the revolver and the cutlass in his belt, and
lit a dark lantern so that it might be ready in case of
need. This done, he left the watch-house, locking the
door behind him, and, after looking steadily across the
Bay to the Scaurs beyond, turned and walked north-
ward towards the Watter's Mou'. Between the cliff on
the edge of this and the watch-house there was a crane
used for raising the granite boulders quarried below,
and when he drew near this he stopped instinctively
and called out, "Who is there?" for he felt, rather than
saw, some presence. "It is only me, Willy," came a soft
voice, and a woman drew a step nearer through the
darkness from behind the shaft of the crane.

"Maggie! Why, darling, what brings you here? I
thought you were going to the wedding!"

"I knew ye wadna be there, and I wanted to speak

wi' ye" — this was said in a very low voice.

"How did you know I wouldn't be there? — I was to join you if I could."

"I saw Bella Cruickshank hand ye the telegram as ye went by the Post Office, and — and I knew there would be something to keep ye. O Willy, Willy! why do ye draw awa frae me?" for Sailor Willy had instinctively loosened his arms which were round her and had drawn back — in the instant his love and his business seemed as though antagonistic. He answered with blunt truthfulness:

"I was thinking, Maggie, that I had no cause to be making love here and now. I've got work, mayhap, tonight!"

"I feared so, Willy — I feared so!" Willy was touched, for it seemed to him that she was anxious for him, and answered tenderly:

"All right, dear! All right! There's no danger — why, if need be, I am armed," and he slipped his hand on the butt of the revolver in his belt. To his surprise Maggie uttered a deep low groan, and turning away sat on the turf bank beside her, as though her strength was failing her. Willy did not know what to say, so there was a space of silence. Then Maggie went on hurriedly:

"Oh my God! it is a dreadfu' thing to lift yer han' in sic a deadly manner against yer neighbors, and ye not knowing what woe ye mau cause." Willy could answer this time:

"Ah, lass! it's hard indeed, and that's the truth. But that's the very reason that men like me are put here that can and will do their duty no matter how hard it may be."

Another pause, and then Maggie spoke again. Willy could not see her face, but she seemed to speak between gasps for breath.

"Ye're lookin' for hard wark the nicht?"

"I am! — I fear so."

"I can guess that that telegram tellt ye that some boats would try to rin in somewhere the nicht."

"Mayhap, lass. But the telegrams are secret, and I must not speak of what's in them."

After a long pause Maggie spoke again, but in a voice so low that he could hardly hear her amid the roar of the breaking waves that came in on the wind:

"Willy, ye're not a cruel man! — ye wadna, if ye could help it, dae harm to them that loved ye, or work woe to their belongin's?"

"My lass! that I wouldn't." As he answered he felt a horrible sinking of the heart. What did all this mean? Was it possible that Maggie, too, had any interest in the smuggling? No, no! a thousand times no! Ashamed of his suspicion he drew closer and again put his arm around her in a protecting way. The unexpected tenderness overcame her, and, bursting into tears, she threw herself on Willy's neck and whispered to him between her sobs:

"O Willy, Willy! I'm in sic sair trouble, and there's nane that I can speak to. Nae! not ane in the wide warld."

"Tell me, darling; you know you'll soon be my wife, and then I'll have a right to know all!"

"Oh, I canna! I canna! I canna!" she said, and taking her arms from around his neck she beat her hands wildly together. Willy was something frightened, for a woman's distress touches a strong man in direct ratio to his manliness. He tried to soothe her as though she were a frightened child, and held her tight to him.

"There! there! my darling. Don't cry. I'm here with you, and you can tell me all your trouble." She shook her head; he felt the movement on his breast, and he went on:

"Don't be frightened, Maggie; tell me all. Tell me quietly, and mayhap I can help ye out over the difficult places." Then he remained silent, and her sobs grew less violent; at last she raised her head and dashed away her tears fiercely with her hand. She dragged herself away from him: he tried to stop her, but she said:

"Nae, nae, Willy dear; let me speak it in my ain way. If I canna trust ye, wha can I trust? My trouble is not for mysel." She paused, and he asked:

"Who, then, is it for?"

"My father and my brothers." Then she went on hurriedly, fearing to stop lest her courage should fail her, and he listened in dead silence, with a growing pain in his heart.

"Ye ken that for several seasons back our boat has had bad luck — we took less fish and lost mair nets than any of the boats; even on the land everything went wrong. Our coo died, and the shed was blawn doon, and then the blight touched the potatoes in our field. Father could dae naething, and had to borrow money on the boat to go on with his wark; and the debt grew and grew, till now he only owns her in name, and we never ken when we may be sold up. And the man that has the mortgage isn't like to let us off or gie time!"

"Who is he? His name?" said Willy hoarsely.

"Mendoza — the man frae Hamburg wha lends to the boats at Peterhead."

Willy groaned. Before his eyes rose the vision of that hard, cruel, white face that he had seen only a few minutes ago, and again he saw him hand over the presents with which he had bought the man and woman to help in his wicked scheme. When Maggie heard the groan her courage and her hope arose. If her lover could take the matter so much to heart all might

yet be well, and in the moment all the womanhood in
her awoke to the call. Her fear had broken down the
barriers that had kept back her passion, and now the
passion came with all the force of a virgin nature. She
drew Willy close to her — closer still — and whispered
to him in a low sweet voice, that thrilled with emotion:

"Willy, Willy, darlin'; ye wouldna see harm come to
my father — my father, my father!" and in a wave of
tumultuous, voluptuous passion she kissed him full in
the mouth. Willy felt for the moment half dazed. Love
has its opiates that soothe and stun even in the midst
of their activity. He clasped Maggie close in his arms,
and for a moment their hearts beat together and their
mouths breathed the same air. Then Willy drew back,
but Maggie hung limp in his arms. The silence that
hung in the midst of nature's tumult broke its own
spell. Willy realized what and where he was: with the
waves dashing below his feet and the night wind laden
with drifting mist wreathing around him in the darkness, and whistling amongst the rocks and screaming
sadly through the ropes and stays of the flagstaff on
the cliff. There was a wild fear in his heart and a
burning desire to know all that was in his sweetheart's
mind.

"Go on, Maggie! go on!" he said. Maggie roused
herself and again took up the thread of her story — this
time in feverish haste. The moment of passion had
disquieted and disturbed her. She seemed to herself to
be two people, one of whom was new to her, and whom
she feared, but womanlike, she felt that as she had
begun so much she go on; and thus her woman's
courage sustained her.

"Some weeks ago, father began to get letters frae Mr.
Mendoza, and they aye upset him. He wrote answers
and sent them away at once. Then Mr. Mendoza sent

him a telegram frae Hamburg, and he sent a reply — and a month ago father got a telegram telling him to meet him at Peterhead. He was very angry at first and very low-spirited after; but he went to Peterhead, and when he cam back he was very still and quite pale. He would eat naething, and went to bed although it was only seven o'clock. Then there were more letters and telegrams, but father answered nane o' them — sae far as I ken — and then Mr. Mendoza cam to our hoose. Father got as pale as a sheet when he saw him, and then he got red and angry, and I thocht he was going to strike him; but Mr. Mendoza said not to frichten his daughter, and father got quiet and sent me oot on a message to the Nether Mill. And when I cam back Mr. Mendoza had gone, and father was sitting with his face in his hands, and he didna hear me come in. When I spoke, he started up and he was as white as a sheet, and then he mumbled something and went into his room. And ever since then he hardly spoke to any one, and seemed to avoid me a'thegither. When he went away the last time he never even kissed me. And so, Willy — so, I fear that that awfu' Mr. Mendoza has made him dae something that he didna want to dae, and it's all breaking my heart!" and again she laid her head on her lover's breast and sobbed. Willy breathed more freely; but he could not be content to remain in doubt, and his courage was never harder tried than when he asked his next question.

"Then, Maggie, you don't know anything for certain?"

"Naething, Willy — but I fear."

"But there may be nothing, after all!" Maggie's hopes rose again, for there was something in her lover's voice which told her that he was willing to cling to any straw, and once again her woman's nature took advantage of her sense of right and wrong. "Please God, Willy, there may be naething! but I fear much that it may be so; but we must act as if we didna fear. It wadna dae to suspect poor father without some cause. You know, Willy, the Earl has promised to mak him the new harbormaster. Old Forgie is bedridden now, and when winter comes he'll no even be able to pretend to work, so the Earl is to pension him, and father will get the post and hae the hoose by the harbor, and you know that every one's sae glad, for they a'respect father."

"Aye, lass," interrupted Willy, "that's true; and why, then, should we — you and me, Maggie — think he would do ill to please that damned scoundrel, Mendoza?"

"Indeed, I'm thinkin' that it's just because that he is respeckit that Mendoza wants him to help him. He kens weel that nane would suspeck father, and —" here she clipped her lover close in her arms once again, and her breath came hot in his face till it made him half drunk with a voluptuous intoxication "— he kens that father, my father, would never be harmt by my lover!"

Even then, at the moment when the tragedy of his life seemed to be accomplished, when the woman he loved and honored seemed to be urging him to some breach of duty, Willy Barrow could not but feel that some responsibility for her action rested on him. That first passionate kiss, which had seemed to unlock the very gates of her soul — in which she had yielded herself to him — had some mysterious bond or virtue like that which abides in the wedding ring. The Maggie who thus acted was his Maggie, and in all that came of it he had a part. But his mind was made up; nothing — not Maggie's kisses or Maggie's fears — would turn him from his path of duty, and strong in this resolution he could afford to be silent to the woman in his arms.

Maggie instinctively knew that silence could now be her best weapon, and said no word as they walked towards the guardhouse, Willy casting keen looks seawards, and up and down the coast as they went. When they were so close that in its shelter the roar of the surf seemed muffled, Maggie again nestled close to her lover, and whispered in his ear as he looked out over Cruden Bay:

"The Sea Gull comes hame the nicht!" Willy quivered, but said nothing for a time that seemed to be endless. Then he answered — "They'll find it hard to make the Port tonight. Look! the waves are rolling high and the wind is getting up. It would be madness to try it." Again she whispered to him:

"Couldna she rin in somewhere else — there are other openings besides Port Erroll in Buchan!" Willy laughed the laugh of a strong man who knew well what he said:

"Other openings! Aye, lass, there are other openings; but the coble isn't built that can run them this night. With a southeast gale, who would dare to try? The Bullers, or Robies Haven, or Dunbuy, or Twa Havens, or Lang Haven, or The Watter's Mou' — why, lass, they'd be in matches on the rocks before they could turn their tiller or slack a sail."

She interrupted him, speaking with a despairing voice:

"Then ye'll no hae to watch nane o' them the nicht?"

"Nay, Maggie. Port Erroll is my watch tonight; and from it I won't budge."

"And the Watter's Mou'?" she asked, "it that no safe wi'oot watch? it's no far frae the Port." Again Willy laughed his arrogant, masculine laugh, which made Maggie, despite her trouble, admire him more than ever, and he answered:

"The Watter's Mou'? To try to get in there in this wind would be to court sudden death. Why, lass, it would take a man all he knew to get out from there, let alone get in, in this weather! And then the chances would be ten to one that he'd be dashed to pieces on the rocks beyond," and he pointed to where a line of sharp rocks rose between the billows on the south side of the inlet. Truly it was a fearful-looking place to be dashed on, for the great waves broke on the rocks with a loud roaring, and even in the semi-darkness they could see the white lines as the waters poured down to leeward in the wake of the heaving wave. The white cluster of rocks looked like a ghostly mouth opened to swallow whatever might come in touch. Maggie shuddered; but some sudden idea seemed to strike her, and she drew away from her lover for a moment, and looked towards the black cleft in the rocks of which they could just see the top from where they stood — the entrance to the Watter's Mou'.

And then with one long, wild, appealing glance skyward, as though looking a prayer that she dared not utter even in her heart, Maggie turned towards her lover once more. Again she drew close to him, and hung around his neck, and said with many gasps and pauses between her words:

"If the Sea Gull should come in to the Port the nicht, and if ony attempt that ye feared should tak you away to Whinnyfold or to Dunbuy so that you might be a bit — only a wee bit — late to search when the boat cam in —"

She stopped affrighted, for Willy put her from him to arm's length, not too gently either, and said to her so sternly that each word seemed to smite her like the lash of a whip, till she shrunk and quivered and cowered away from him:

"Maggie, lass! What's this you're saying to me? It isn't fit for you to speak or me to hear! It's bad enough to be a smuggler, but what is it that you would make of me? Not only a smuggler, but a perjurer and a traitor too. God! am I mistaken? Is it you, Maggie, that would make this of me? Of me! Maggie MacWhirter, if this be your counsel, then God help us both! you are no fit wife for me!" In an instant the whole truth dawned on Maggie of what a thing she would make of the man she loved, whom she had loved at the first because he was strong and brave and true. In the sudden revulsion of her feelings she flung herself on her knees beside him, and took his hand and held it hard, and despite his efforts to withdraw it, kissed it wildly in the humility of her self-abasement, and poured out to him a passionate outburst of pleading for his forgiveness, of justification of herself, and of appeals to his mercy for her father.

"Oh Willy, Willy! dinna turn frae me this nicht! My heart is sae fu' o' trouble that I am nigh mad! I dinna ken what to dae nor where to look for help! I think, and think, and think, and everywhere there is nought but dark before me, just as there is blackness oot ower the sea, when I look for my father. And noo when I want ye to help me — ye that are all I hae, and the only ane on earth that I can look tae in my wae and trouble — I can dae nae mair than turn ye frae me! Ye that I love! oh, love more than my life or my soul! I must dishonor and mak ye hate me! Oh, what shall I dae? What shall I dae? What shall I dae?" and again she beat the palms of her hands together in a paroxysm of wild despair, whilst Willy looked on with his heart full of pain and pity, though his resolution never flinched. And then through the completeness of her self-abasement came the pleading of her soul from a depth of her nature even deeper than despair. Despair has its own bravery, but hope can sap the strongest resolution. And the pleadings of love came from the depths of that Pandora's box which we call human nature.

"O Willy, Willy! forgie me — forgie me! I was daft to say what I did! I was daft to think that ye would be so base! — daft to think that I would like you to so betray yoursel! Forgie me, Willy, forgie me, and tak my wild words as spoken not to ye but to the storm that maks me fear sae for my father! Let me tak it a' back, Willy darlin' — Willy, my Willy; and dinna leave me desolate here with this new shadow ower me!" Here, as she kissed his hand again, her lover stooped and raised her in his strong arms and held her to him. And then, when she felt herself in a position of security, the same hysterical emotion came sweeping up in her brain and her blood — the same self-abandonment to her lover overcame her — and the current of her thought once again turned to win from him something by the force of her woman's wile and her woman's contact with the man.

"Willy," she whispered, as she kissed him on the mouth and then kissed his head on the side of his neck, "Willy, ye have forgien me, I ken — and I ken that ye'll harm father nae mair than ye can help — but if —"

What more she was going to say she hardly knew herself. As for Willy, he felt that something better left unsaid was coming, and unconsciously his muscles stiffened till he held her from him rather than to him. She, too, felt the change, and held him closer — closer still, with the tenacity induced by a sense of coming danger. Their difficulty was solved for them, for just on the instant when the suggestion of treachery to his duty was hanging on her lips, there came from the village below, in a pause between the gusts of wind, the fierce roar of a flying rocket. Up and up and up, as though it would never stop — up it rose with its prolonged screech, increasing in sound at the first till it began to die away in the aerial heights above, so that when the explosion came it seemed to startle a quietude around it. Up in the air a thousand feet over their heads the fierce glitter of the falling fires of red and blue made a blaze of light which lit up the coastline from the Scaurs to Dunbuy, and with an instinctive intelligence Willy Barrow took in all he saw, including the many men at the little port below, sheltering under the sea-wall from the sweeping of the waves as they looked out seawards. Instinctively also he counted the seconds till the next rocket should be fired — one, two, three; and then another roar and another blaze of colored lights. And then another pause, of six seconds this time! and then the third rocket sped aloft with its fiery message. And then the darkness seemed blacker than ever, and the mysterious booming of the sea to grow louder and louder as though it came through silence. By this time the man and the woman were apart no less in spirit than physically. Willy, intent on his work, was standing outside the window of the guard-house, whence he could see all around the Bay and up and down the coast, and at the same time command the whole of the harbor. His feet were planted wide apart, for on the exposed rock the sweep of the wind was strong, and as he raised his arm with his field-glass to search the horizon the wind drove back his jacket and showed the butt of his revolver and the hilt of his cutlass. Maggie stood a little behind him, gazing seawards, with no less eager eyes, for she too expected what would follow. Her heart seemed to stand still though her breath came in quick gasps, and she did not dare to make a sound or to encroach on the businesslike earnestness of the man. For full a minute they waited thus, and then far off at sea, away to the south, they saw a faint blue light, and then another and another, till at the last three lights were burning in a row. Instantly from the town a single rocket went up — not this time a great Board of Trade rocket, laden with colored fire, but one that left a plain white track of light behind it. Willy gazed seawards, but there was no more sign from the far-off ship at sea; the signal, whatever it was, was complete. The coastguard was uncertain as to the meaning, but to Maggie no explanation was necessary. There, away at sea, tossed on the stormy waters, was her father. There was danger round him, but a greater danger on the shore — every way of entrance was barred by the storm — save the one where, through his fatal cargo, dishonor lay in wait for him. She seemed to see her duty clear before her, and come what might she meant to do it: her father must be warned. It was with a faint voice indeed that she now spoke to her lover:

"Willy!"

His heart was melted at the faltering voice, but he feared she was trying some new temptation, so, coldly and hardly enough, he answered:

"What is it, lass?"

"Willy, ye wadna see poor father injured?"

"No, Maggie, not if I could help it. But I'd have to do my duty all the same."

"And we should a' dae oor duty — whatever it might be — at a' costs?"

"Aye, lass — at all costs!" His voice was firm enough now, and there was no mistaking the truth of its ring. Maggie's hope died away. From the stern task that seemed to rise before her over the waste of the black sea she must not shrink. There was but one more yielding to the weakness of her fear, and she said, so timidly that Willy was startled, the voice and manner were so different from those he had ever known:

"And if — mind I say 'if', Willy — I had a duty to dae and it was fu' o' fear and danger, and ye could save me frae it, wad ye?" As she waited for his reply, her heart beat so fast and so heavily that Willy could hear it: her very life, she felt, lay in his answer. He did not quite understand the full import of her words and all that they implied, but he knew that she was in deadly earnest, and he felt that some vague terror lay in his answer; but the manhood in him rose to the occasion — Willy Barrow was of the stuff of which heroes are made — and he replied:

"Maggie, as God is above us, I have no other answer to give! I don't know what you mean, but I have a shadow of fear! I must do my duty whatever comes of it!" There was a long pause, and then Maggie spoke again, but this time in so different a voice that her lover's heart went out to her in tenfold love and passion, with never a shadow of doubt or fear.

"Willy, tak me in your arms — I am not unworthy, dear, though for a moment I did falter!" He clasped her to him, and whispered when their lips had met:

"Maggie, my darling, I never loved you like now. I would die for you if I could do you good."

"Hush, dear, I ken it weel. But your duty is not only for yoursel, and it must be done! I too hae a duty to dae — a grave and stern ane!"

"What is it? Tell me, Maggie dear!"

"Ye maunna ask me! Ye maun never ken! Kiss me once again, Willy, before I go — for oh, my love, my love! it may be the last!"

Her words were lost in the passionate embrace that followed. Then, when he least expected it, she suddenly tore herself away and fled through the darkness across the field that lay between them and her home, whilst he stood doggedly at his watch looking out for another signal between sea and shore.

III

hen she got to the far side of the field, Maggie, instead of turning to the left, which would have brought her home, went down the sloping track to the right, which led to the rustic bridge crossing the Back Burn near the Pigeon Tower. Thence turning to the right she scrambled down the bank beside the ruined barley-mill, so as to reach the little plots of sea-grass — islands, except at low tide — between which the tide rises to meet the waters of the stream.

The whole situation of Cruden is peculiar. The main stream, the Water of Cruden, runs in a southeasterly direction, skirts the sand hills, and, swirling under the stone bridge, partly built with the ruins of the old church which Malcolm erected to celebrate his victory over Sueno, turns suddenly to the right and runs to sea over a stony bottom. The estuary has in its wash some dangerous outcropping granite rocks, nearly covered at high tide, and the mouth opens between the most northerly end of the sand hills and the village street, whose houses mark the slope of the detritus from the rocks. Formerly the Water of Cruden, instead of taking this last turn, used to flow straight on till it joined the lesser stream known as the Back Burn, and together the streams ran seawards. Even in comparatively recent years, in times of flood or freshet, the spate broke down or swept over the intervening tongue of land, and the Water of Cruden took its old course seaward. This course is what is known as the Watter's Mou'. It is a natural cleft — formed by primeval fire or earthquake or some sort of natural convulsion — which runs through the vast mass of red granite that forms a promontory running due south. Water has done its work as well as fire in the formation of the gully as it now is, for the drip and flow and rush of water that mark the seasons for countless ages have completed the work of the pristine fire. As one sees this natural mouth of the stream in the rocky face of the cliff, it is hard to realize that Nature alone has done the work.

At first the cleft runs from west to east, and broadens out into a wide bay of which on one side a steep grassy slope leads towards the new castle of Slains, and on the other rises a sheer bank, with tufts of the thick grass growing on the ledges, where the earth has been blown. From this the cleft opens again between towering rocks like what in America is called a canon and tends seaward to the south between precipices two hundred feet high, and over a bottom of great boulders exposed at low water towards the northern end. The precipice to the left or eastward side is twice rent with great openings, through which, in time of storm, the spray and spume of the easterly gale piling the great waves into the Castle Bay are swept. These openings are, however, so guarded with masses of rock that the force of the wildest wave is broken before it can leap up the piles of boulders that rise from their sandy floors. At the very mouth the cleft opens away to the west, where the cliff falls back, and seaward of which rise great masses of black frowning rock, most of which only show their presence at high water by the angry patches of foam which even in calm weather mark them — for the current here runs fast. The eastern portal is composed of a giant mass of red granite, which, from its overhanging shape, is known as "the Ship's Starn." It lies somewhat lower than the cliff of which it is a part, being attached to it by a great sloping shelf of granite, over which, when the storm is easterly, the torrent of spray sent up by the dashing waves rolls down to join the foamy waves in the Watter's Mou'.

Maggie knew that close to the Barley Mill, safe from the onset of the waves — for the wildest waves that ever rise lose their force fretting and churning on the stony sides and bottom of the Watter's Mou' — was kept a light boat belonging to her brother, which he sometimes used when the weather was fine and he wanted to utilize his spare time in line fishing. Her mind was made up that it was her duty to give her father warning of what awaited him on landing — if she could. She was afraid to think of the danger, of the myriad chances against her success; but, womanlike, when once the idea was fixed in her mind she went straight on to its realization. Truly, thought of any kind would have been an absolute barrier to action in such a case, for any one of the difficulties ahead would have seemed sufficient. To leave the shore at all on such a night, and in such a frail craft, with none but a girl to manage it; then to find a way, despite storm and current, out to the boat so far off at sea; and finally, to find the boat she wanted at all in the fret of such a stormy sea — a wilderness of driving mist — in such a night, when never a star even was to be seen: the prospect might well appall the bravest.

But to think was to hesitate, and to hesitate was to fail. Keeping her thoughts on the danger to her father, and seeing through the blackness of the stormy night his white, woe-laden face before her, and hearing through the tumult of the tempest his sobs as on that night when her fear for him began to be acute, she set about her work with desperate energy. The boat was moored on the northern side of the largest of the little islands of sea-grass, and so far in shelter that she could get all in readiness. She set the oars in their places, stepped the mast, and rigged the sail ready to haul up. Then she took a small spar of broken wood and knotted to it a piece of rope, fastening the other end of the rope, some five yards long, just under the thwarts near the center of the boat, and just a little forward on the port side. The spar she put carefully ready to throw out of the boat when the sweep of the wind should take her sail — for without some such strain as it would afford, the boat would probably heel over. Then she guided the boat in the shallow water round the little island till it was stern on to the seaside. It was rough work, for the rush and recoil of the waves beat the boat back on the sandy bank or left her now and again dry till a new wave lifted her.

All this time she took something of inspiration from the darkness and the roar of the storm around her. She was not yet face to face with danger, and did not realize, or try to realize, its magnitude. In such a mystery of darkness as lay before, above, and around her, her own personality seemed as naught. Truly there is an instinct of one's own littleness that becomes consciously manifest in the times when Nature puts forth her might. The wind swept up the channel of the Watter's Mou' in great gusts, till the open bay where she stood became the center of an intermittent whirlwind. The storm came not only from the Mouth itself, but through the great gaps in the eastern wall. It drove across the gully till high amongst the rocks overhead on both sides it seemed now and again to scream as a living thing in pain or anger. Great sheets of mist appeared out of the inky darkness beyond, coming suddenly as though like the great sails of ships driving up before the wind. With gladness Maggie saw that the sheets of fog were becoming fewer and thinner, and realized that so far her dreadful task was becoming possible. She was getting more inspired by the sound and elemental fury around her. There was in her blood, as in the blood of all the hardy children of the northern seas, some strain of those study Berserkers who knew no fear, and rode the very tempest on its wings with supreme bravery. Such natures rise with the occasion, and now, when the call had come, Maggie's brave nature answered it. It was with a strong, almost an eager, heart that she jumped into the boat, and seizing the oars, set out on her perilous course. The start was difficult, for the boat was bumping savagely on the sand; but, taking advantage of a big wave, two or three powerful strokes took her out into deeper water. Here, too, there was shelter, for the cliffs rose steeply; and when she had entered the elbow of the gully and saw before her the whole length of the Watter's Mou', the drift of the wind took it over her head, and she was able to row in comparative calmness under the shadow of the cliffs. A few minutes took her to the first of the openings in the eastern cliff, and here she began to feel the full fury of the storm. The opening itself was sheer on each side, but in the gap between was piled a mass of giant boulders, the work of the sea at its wildest during the centuries of stress. On the farther side of these the waves broke, and sent up a white cloud of spume that drove instantly into the darkness beyond. Maggie knew that here her first great effort had to be made, and lending her strength pulled the boat through the turmoil of wind and wave. As she passed the cleft, driven somewhat more out into the middle of the channel, she caught, in a pause between the rush of the waves, a glimpse of the lighted windows of the castle on the cliff. The sight for an instant unnerved her, for it brought into opposition her own dreadful situation, mental and physical, with the happy faces of those clustered round the comforting light. But the reaction was helpful, for the little jealousy that was at the base of the idea was blotted out by the thought of that stem and paramount duty which she had undertaken. Not seldom in days gone by had women like her, in times of test and torment, taken their way over the red-hot ploughshares under somewhat similar stress of mind.

She was now under the shelter of the cliff, and gaining the second and last opening in the rocky wall: as the boat advanced the force of the waves became greater, for every yard up the Watter's Mou' the fretting of the rocky bottom and sides had broken their force. This was brought home to her roughly when the breaking of a coming wave threw a sheet of water over her as she bent to her oars. Chop! chop! went the boat into the trough of each succeeding wave, till it became necessary to bale out the boat or she might never even get started on her way. This done she rowed on, and now came to the second opening in the cliff. This was much wilder than the first, for outside of it, to the east, the waves of the North Sea broke in all their violence, and with the breaking of each a great sheet of water came drifting over the wall of piled up boulders. Again Maggie kept out in the channel, and, pulling with all her might, passed again into the shelter of the cliff. Here the water was stiller, for the waves were breaking directly behind the sheltering cliff, and the sound of them was heard high overhead in the rushing wind.

Maggie drew close to the rock, and, hugging it, crept on her outward way. There was now only one danger to come, before her final effort. The great shelf of rock inside the Ship's Starn was only saved from exposure by its rise on the outer side; but here, happily, the waves did not break, they swept under the overhanging slope on the outer side, and then passed on their way; the vast depth of the water outside was their protection within. Now and then a wave broke on the edge of the Ship's Starn, and then a great wall of green water rose and rushed down the steep slope, but in the pause between Maggie passed along; and now the boat nestled on the black water, under the shelter of the very outermost wall of rock. The Ship's Starn was now her last refuge. As she hurriedly began to get the sail ready she could hear the whistling of the wind round the outer side of the rock and overhead. The black water underneath her rose and fell, but in some mysterious eddy or backwater of Nature's forces she rested in comparative calm on the very edge of the maelstrom. By contrast with the darkness of the Watter's Mou' between the towering walls of rock, the sea had some mysterious light of its own, and just outside the opening on the western side she could see the white water pouring over the sunken rocks as the passing waves exposed them, till once more they looked like teeth in the jaws of the hungry sea.

And now came the final struggle in her effort to get out to open water. The moment she should pass beyond the shelter of the Ship's Starn the easterly gale would in all probability drive her straight upon the outer reef of rocks amongst those angry jaws, where the white teeth would in an instant grind her and her boat to nothingness. But if she should pass this last danger she should be out in the open sea and might make her way to save her father. She held in her mind the spot whence she had seen the answering signal to the rockets, and felt a blind trust that God would help her in her difficulty. Was not God pleased with self-sacrifice? What could be better for a maid than to save her father from accomplished sin and the discovery that made sin so bitter to bear? "Greater love hath no man than this, that a man lay down his life for his friend." Besides there was Sailor Willy! Had not he — even he — doubted her; and might she not by this wild night's work win back her old place in his heart and his faith? Strong in this new hope, she made careful preparation for her great effort. She threw overboard the spar and got ready the tiller. Then having put the sheet round the thwart on the starboard side, and laid the loose end where she could grasp it whilst holding the tiller, she hoisted the sail and belayed the rope that held it. In the eddy of the storm behind the sheltered rock the sail hung idly for a few seconds, and in this time she jumped to the stern and held the tiller with one hand and with the other drew the sheet of the sail taut and belayed it. An instant after, the sail caught a gust of wind and the boat sprang, as though a living thing, out toward the channel. The instant the shelter was past the sail caught the full sweep of the easterly gale, and the boat would have turned over only for the strain from the floating spar line, which now did its part well. The bow was thrown round towards the wind, and the boat began rushing through the water at a terrific pace. Maggie felt the coldness of death in her heart; but in that wild moment the bravery of her nature came out. She shut her teeth and jammed the tiller down hard, keeping it in place against her thigh, with the other leg pressed like a pillar against the side of the boat. The little craft seemed sweeping right down on the outer rocks; already she could see the white wall of water, articulated into white lines like giant hairs, rushing after the retreating waves, and a great despair swept over her. But at that moment the rocks on the western side of the Watter's Mou' opened so far that she caught a glimpse of Sailor Willy's lamp reflected through the window of the coastguard hut. This gave her new hope, and with a mighty effort she pressed the tiller harder. The boat sank in the trough of the waves, rose again, the spar caught the rush of the receding wave and pulled the boat's head a point round, and then the outer rock was passed, and the boat, actually touching the rock so that the limpets scraped her side, ran free in the stormy waves beyond.

Maggie breathed a prayer as with trembling hand she unloosed the rope of the floating spar; then, having loosened the sheet, she turned the boat's head south, and, tacking, ran out in the direction where she had seen the signal light of her father's boat.

By contrast with the terrible turmoil amid the rocks, the great waves of the open sea were safety itself. No one to whom the sea is an occupation ever fears it in the open; and this fisher's daughter, with the Viking blood in her veins, actually rejoiced as the cockleshell of a boat, dipping and jerking like an angry horse, drove up and down the swell of the waves. She was a good way out now, and the whole coastline east and west was opening up to her. The mist had gone by, or, if it lasted, hung amid the rocks inshore; and through the great blackness round she saw the lights in the windows of the castle, the glimmering lights of the village of Cruden, and far off the powerful light at Girdleness blazing out at intervals. But there was one light on which her eyes lingered fixedly — the dim window of the coastguard's shelter, where she knew that her lover kept his grim watch. Her heart was filled with gladness as she thought that by what she was doing she would keep pain and trouble from him. She knew now, what she had all along in her heart believed, that Sailor Willy would not flinch from any duty however stern and pain-laden to him it might be; and she knew, too, that neither her rugged father nor her passionate young brother would ever forgive him for that duty. But now she would not, could not, think of failing, but gripped the tiller hard, and with set teeth and fixed eyes held on her perilous way.

Time went by hour by hour, but so great was her anxiety that she never noted how it went, but held on her course, tacking again and again as she tried to beat her way to her father through the storm. The eyes of sea folk are not ordinary eyes — they can pierce the darkness wherein the vision of land folk becomes lost or arrested; and the sea and the sky over it, and the coastline, however black and dim — however low-lying or distant — have lessons of their own. Maggie began by some mysterious instinct to find her way where she wanted to go, till little by little the coastline, save for the distant lights of Girdleness and Boddam, faded out of sight. Lying as she was on the very surface of the water, she had the horizon rising as it were around her, and there is nearly always some slight sign of light somewhere on the horizon's rim. There came now and again rents in the thick clouding of the stormy sky, and at such moments here and there came patches of lesser darkness like oases of light in the desert of the ebon sea. At one such moment she saw far off to the port side the outline of a vessel well known on the coast, the revenue cutter that was the seaward arm of the preventive service. And then a great fear came over poor Maggie's heart; the sea was no longer the open sea, for her father was held in the toils of his enemies, and escape seaward became difficult or would be almost impossible, when the coming morn would reveal all the mysteries that the darkness hid. Despair, however, has its own courage, and Maggie was too far in her venture now to dread for more than a passing moment anything that might follow. She knew that the Sea Gull lay still to the front, and with a beating heart and a brain that throbbed with the eagerness of hope and fear she held on her course. The break in the sky that had shown her the revenue cutter was only momentary, and all was again swallowed up in the darkness; but she feared that some other such rent in the cloudy night might expose her father to his enemies. Every moment, therefore, became precious, and steeling her heart and drawing the sheet of her sail as tight as she dared, she sped on into the darkness — on for a time that seemed interminable agony. Suddenly something black loomed up ahead of her, thrown out against the light of the horizon's rim, and her heart gave a great jump, for something told her that the Powers which aid the good wishes of daughters had sent her father out of that wilderness of stormy sea. With her sea-trained eyes she knew in a few moments that the boat pitching so heavily was indeed the Sea

Gull. At the same moment some one on the boat's deck saw her sail, and a hoarse muffled murmur of voices came to her over the waves in the gale. The coble's head was thrown round to the wind, and in that stress of storm and chopping sea she beat and buffeted, and like magic her way stopped, and she lay tossing. Maggie realized the intention of the maneuver, and deftly swung her boat round till she came under the starboard quarter of the fishing-boat, and in the shadow of her greater bulk and vaster sail, reefed though it was, found a comparative calm. Then she called out:

"Father! It's me — Maggie! Dinna show a licht, but try to throw me a rope."

With a shout in which were mingled many strong feelings, her father leaned over the bulwark, and, with seaman's instinct of instant action, threw her a rope. She deftly caught it, and, making it fast to the bows of her boat, dropped her sail. Then someone threw her another rope, which she fastened round her waist. She threw herself into the sea, and, holding tight to the rope, was shortly pulled breathless on board the Sea Gull.

She was instantly the center of a ring of men. Not only were her father and two brothers on board, but there were no less than six men, seemingly foreigners, in the group.

"Maggie!" said her father, "in God's name, lass, hoo cam ye oot here? Were ye ovrta'en by the storm? God be thankit that ye met us, for this is a wild nicht to be oot on the North Sea by yer lanes."

"Father!" said she, in a hurried whisper in his ear. "I must speak wi' ye alane. There isna a moment to lose!"

"Speak on, lass."

"No' before these strangers, father. I must speak alane!" Without a word, MacWhirter took his daughter aside, and, amid a muttered dissatisfaction of the strange men, signed to her to proceed. Then, as briefly as she could, Maggie told her father that it was known that a cargo was to be run that night, that the coast-guard all along Buchan had been warned, and that she had come out to tell him of his danger.

As she spoke the old man groaned, and after a pause said: "I maun tell the rest. I'm no' the maister here the noo. Mendoza has me in his grip, an' his men rule here!"

"But, father, the boat is yours, and the risk is yours. It is you'll be punished if there is a discovery!"

"That may be, lass, but I'm no' free."

"I feared it was true, father, but I thocht it my duty to come!" Doubtless the old man knew that Maggie would understand fully what he meant, but the only recognition he made of her act of heroism was to lay his hand heavily on her shoulder. Then stepping forward he called the men round him, and in his own rough way told them of the danger. The strangers muttered and scowled; but Andrew and Neil drew close to their sister, and the younger man put his arm around her and pressed her to him. Maggie felt the comfort of the kindness, and laying her head on her brother's shoulder, cried quietly in the darkness. It was a relief to her pent-up feelings to be able to give way if only so far. When MacWhirter brought his tale to a close, and asked: "And now, lads, what's to be done?" one of the strangers, a brawny, heavily-built man, spoke out harshly:

"But for why this? Was it not that this woman's lover was of the guard? In this affair the women must do their best too. This lover of the guard —" He was hotly interrupted by Neil:

"'Tisna the part of Maggie to tak a hand in this at

a'."

"But I say it is the part of all. When Mendoza bought this man he bought all — unless there be traitors in his housed!" This roused Maggie, who spoke out quickly, for she feared her brother's passion might brew trouble:

"I hae nae part in this dreadfu' affair. It's no' by ma wish or ma aid that father has embarked in this — this enterprise. I hae naught to dae wi't o' ony kind."

"Then for why are you here?" asked the burly man, with a coarse laugh.

"Because ma father and ma brithers are in danger, danger into which they hae been led, or been forced, by ye and the like o' ye. Do you think it was for pleasure, or, O my God! for profit either, that I cam oot this nicht — an' in that?" and as she spoke she pointed to where the little boat strained madly at the rope which held her. Then MacWhirter spoke out fiercely, so fiercely that the lesser spirits who opposed him were cowed:

"Leave the lass alane, I say! Yon's nane o' her doin'; and if ye be men ye'd honor her that cam oot in sic a tempest for the sake o' the likes o' me — o' us!"

But when the strangers were silent, Neil, whose passion had been aroused, could not be quietened, and spoke out with a growing fury which seemed to choke him:

"So Sailor Willy told ye the danger and then let ye come oot in this nicht! He'll hae to reckon wi' me for that when we get in."

"He telt me naething. I saw Bella Cruickshank gie him the telegram, and I guessed. He doesna ken I'm here — and he maun never ken. Nane must ever ken that a warning cam the nicht to father!"

"But they'll watch for us comin' in."

"We maun rin back to Cuxhaven," said the quiet

voice of Andrew, who had not yet spoken."

"But ye canna," said Maggie; "the revenue cutter is on the watch, and when the mornin' comes will follow ye; and besides, hoo can ye get to Cuxhaven in this wind?"

"Then what are we to do, lass?" said her father.

"Dae, father? Dae what ye should dae — throw a' this poisonous stuff that has brought this ruin owerboard. Lichten yer boat as ye will lighten yer conscience, and come hame as ye went oot!"

The burly ran swore a great oath.

"Nothing overboard shall be thrown. These belongs not to you but to Mendoza. If they be touched he closes on your boat and ruin it is for you!" Maggie saw her father hesitate, and feared that other counsels might prevail, so she spoke out as by an inspiration. There, amid the surges of the perilous seas, the daughter's heroic devotion and her passionate earnestness made a new calm in her father's life:

"Father, dinna be deceived. Wi' this wind on shore, an' the revenue cutter ootside an' the dawn no' far off ye canna escape. Noo in the darkness ye can get rid o' the danger. Dinna lose a moment. The storm is somewhat lesser just enoo. Throw a' owerboard and come back to yer old self! What if we be ruined? We can work; and shall a' be happy yet!"

Something seemed to rise in the old man's heart and give him strength. Without pause he said with a grand simplicity:

"Ye're reet, lass, ye're reet! Haud up the casks, men, and stave them in!"

Andrew and Neil rushed to his bedding. Mendoza's men protested, but were afraid to intervene, and one after another bales and casks were lifted on deck. The bales were tossed overboard and the heads of the casks stove in till the scuppers were alternately drenched with brandy and washed with the seas.

In the midst of this, Maggie, knowing that if all were to be of any use she must be found at home in the morning, quietly pulled her boat as close as she dared, and slipping down the rope managed to clamber into it. Then she loosed the painter; and the wind and waves took her each instant farther and farther away. The sky over the horizon was brightening every instant, and there was a wild fear in her heart that not even the dull thud of the hammers as the casks were staved in could allay. She felt that it was a race against time, and her overexcited imagination multiplied her natural fear; her boat's head was to home, steering for where she guessed was the dim light on the cliff, towards which her heart yearned. She hauled the sheets close — as close as she dared, for now speed was everything if she was to get back unseen. Well she knew that Sailor Willy on his lonely vigil would be true to his trust, and that his eagle eye could not fail to note her entry when once the day had broken. In a fever of anxiety she kept her eye on the Girdleness light by which she had to steer, and with the rise and fall of every wave as she swept by them, threw the boat's head a point to the wind and let it fall away again.

The storm had nearly spent itself, but there were still angry moments when the mist was swept in masses before fresh gusts. These, however, were fewer and fewer, and in a little while she ceased to heed them or even to look for them, and at last her eager eye began to discern through the storm the flickering lights of the little port. There came a moment when the tempest poured out the lees of its wrath in one final burst of energy, which wrapped the flying boat in a wraith of mist.

And then the tempest swept onward, shoreward, with the broken mist showing white in the springing dawn like the wings of some messenger of coming peace.

IV

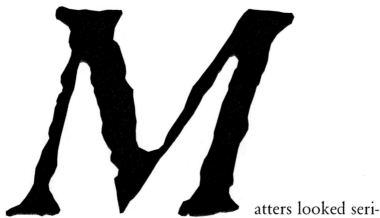atters looked serious enough on the Sea Gull when the time came in which rather the darkness began to disappear than the light to appear. Night and day have their own mysteries, and their nascence is as distant and as mysterious as the origin of life. The sky and the waters still seemed black, and the circle in which the little craft lived was as narrow as ever; but here and there in sky and on sea were faint streaks perceptible rather than distinguishable, as though swept thither by the trumpet blast of the messenger of the dawn. Mendoza's men did not stint their curses nor their threats, and Neil with passionate violence so assailed them in return that both MacWhirter and Andrew had to exercise their powers of restraint. But blood is hot, and the lives of lawless men are prone to make violence a habit; the two elder

69

men were anxious that there should be no extension
of the present bitter bickering. As for MacWhirter, his
mind was in a whirl and tumult of mixed emotions.
First came his anxiety for Maggie when she had set
forth alone on the stormy sea with such inadequate
equipment. Well the old fisherman knew the perils that
lay before her in her effort to win the shore, and his
heart was positively sick with anxiety when every effort
of thought or imagination concerning her ended in
something like despair. In one way he was happier than
he had been for many months; the impending blow
had fallen, and though he was ruined it had come in
such a time that his criminal intent had not been
accomplished. Here again his anxiety regarding Maggie
became intensified, for was it not to save him that she
had set forth on her desperate enterprise. He groaned
aloud as he thought of the price that he might yet have
to pay — that he might have paid already, though he
knew it not as yet — for the service which had saved
him from the after-consequences of his sin. He dared
not think more on the subject, for it would, he feared,
madden him, and he must have other work to engross
his thoughts. Thus it was that the danger of collision
between Neil and Mendoza's men became an anodyne
to his pain. He knew that a quarrel among seamen and
under such conditions would be no idle thing, for they
had all their knives, and with such hot blood on all
sides none would hesitate to use them. The whole of
the smuggled goods had by now been thrown overboard, the tobacco having gone the last, the bales
having been broken up. So heavy had been the cargo
that there was a new danger in that the boat was too
much lightened. As Mendoza had intended that force
as well as fraud was to aid this venture he had not stuck
at trifles. There was no pretence of concealment and

even the ballast had made way for cask and box and bale. The Sea Gull had been only partially loaded at Hamburg, but when out of sight of port her cargo had been completed from other boats that had followed, till, when she started for Buchan, she was almost a solid mass of contraband goods. Mendoza's men felt desperate at this hopeless failure of the venture; and as Neil, too, was desperate, in a different way, there was a grim possibility of trouble on board at any minute.

The coming of the dawn was therefore a welcome relief, for it united — if only for a time — all on board to try to avert a common danger.

Lighter and lighter grew the expanse of sea and sky, until over the universe seemed to spread a cool, pearly grey, against which every object seemed to stand starkly out. The smugglers were keenly on the watch, and they saw, growing more clearly each instant out of the darkness, the black, low-lying hull, short funnel, and tapering spars of the revenue cutter about three or four miles off the starboard quarter. The preventive men seemed to see them at the same time, for there was a manifest stir on board, and the cutter's head was changed. Then MacWhirter knew it was necessary to take some bold course of action, for the Sea Gull lay between two fires, and he made up his mind to run then and there for Port Erroll.

As the Sea Gull drew nearer in to shore the waves became more turbulent, for there is ever a more ordered succession in deep waters than where the onward rush is broken by the undulations of the shore. Minute by minute the dawn was growing brighter, and the shore was opening up. The Sea Gull, lightened of her load, could not with safety be thrown across the wind, and so the difficulty of her tacks was increased. The dawn was just shooting its first rays over the eastern sea when the final effort to win the little port came to be made.

The harbor of Port Erroll is a tiny haven of refuge won from the jagged rocks that bound the eastern side of Cruden Bay. It is sheltered on the northern side by the cliff which runs as far as the Watter's Mou', and separated from the mouth of the Water of Cruden, with its waste of shifting sands, by a high wall of concrete. The harbor faces east, and its first basin is the smaller of the two, the larger opening sharply to the left a little way in. At the best of times it is not an easy matter to gain the harbor, for only when the tide has fairly risen is it available at all, and the rapid tide which runs up from the Scaurs makes in itself a difficulty at such times. The tide was now at three-quarters flood, so that in as far as water was concerned there was no difficulty; but the fierceness of the waves that sent up a wall of white water all along the cliffs looked ominous indeed.

As the Sea Gull drew nearer to the shore, considerable commotion was caused on both sea and land. The revenue cutter dared not approach so close to the shore, studded as it was with sunken rocks, as did the lighter draughted coble; but her commander evidently did not mean to let this be to the advantage of the smuggler. A gun was fired to attract the authorities on shore, and signals were got ready to hoist.

The crowd of strangers who thronged the little port had instinctively hidden themselves behind rock and wall and boat, as the revelation of the dawn came upon them, so that the whole place presented the appearance of a warren when the rabbits are beginning to emerge after a temporary scare. There were not wanting, however, many who stood out in the open, affecting, with what nonchalance they could, a simple business interest at the little port. Sailor Willy was on the cliff between the guardhouse and the Watter's Mou', where he had kept his vigil all the night long. As soon as possible after he had sent out his appeal for help the lieutenant had come over from Collieston with a boatman and three men, and these were now down on the quay waiting for the coming of the Sea Gull. When he had arrived, and had learned the state of things, the lieutenant, who knew of Willy Barrow's relations with the daughter of the suspected man, had kindly ordered him to watch the cliff, whilst he himself with the men would look after the port. When he had first given the order in the presence of the other coastguards, Willy had instinctively drawn himself up as though he felt that he, too, had come under suspicion, so the lieutenant took the earliest opportunity when they were alone of saying to Willy:

"Barrow, I have arranged your duties as I have done, not by any means because I suspect that you would be drawn by your sympathies into any neglect of duty — I know you too well for that — but simply because I want to spare you pain in case things may be as we suspect!"

Willy saluted and thanked him with his eyes as he turned away, for he feared that the fullness of his heart might betray him. The poor fellow was much overwrought. All night long he had paced the cliffs in the dull routine of his duty, with his heart feeling like a lump of lead, and his brain on fire with fear. He knew from the wildness of Maggie's rush away from him that she was bent on some desperate enterprise, and as he had no clue to her definite intentions he could only imagine. He thought and thought until his brain almost began to reel with the intensity of his mental effort; and as he was so placed, tied to the stake of his duty, that he could speak with no one on the subject, he had to endure alone, and in doubt, the darkness of his soul, tortured alike by hopes and fears, through all the long night. At last, however, the pain exhausted itself, and doubt became its own anodyne. Despair has its calms — the backwaters of fears — where the tired imagination may rest awhile before the strife begins anew.

With joy he saw that the storm was slackening with the coming of the dawn; and when the last fierce gust had swept by him, screaming through the rigging of the flagstaff overhead, and sweeping inland the broken fragments of the mist, he turned to the sea, now of a cool grey with the light of the coming dawn, and swept it far and wide with his glass. With gladness — and yet with an ache in his heart which he could not understand — he realized that there was in sight only one coble — the Sea Gull — he knew her well — running for the port, and farther out the hull and smoke, the light spars and swift lines of the revenue cutter, which was evidently following her. He strolled with the appearance of leisureliness, though his heart was throbbing, towards the cliff right over the little harbor, so that he could look down and see from close quarters all that went on. He could not but note the many strangers dispersed about, all within easy distance of a rush to the quay when the boat should land, or the way in which the lieutenant and his men seemed to keep guard over the whole place. As first the figures, the walls of the port, the cranes, the boats, and the distant headlands were silhouetted in black against the background of grey sea and grey sky; but as the dawn came closer each object began to stand out in its natural proportions. All kept growing clearer and yet clearer and more and more thoroughly outlined, till the moment came when the sun, shooting over the horizon, set every living thing whose eyes had been regulated to the strain of the darkness and the twilight blinking and winking in the glory of the full light of day.

Eagerly he searched the faces of the crowd with his glass for Maggie, but he could not see her anywhere, and his heart seemed to sink within him, for well he knew that it must be no ordinary cause which kept Maggie from being one of the earliest on the look-out for her father. Closer and closer came the Sea Gull, running for the port with a speed and recklessness that set both the smugglers and the preventive men all agog. Such haste and such indifference to danger sprang, they felt, from no common cause, and they all came to the conclusion that the boat, delayed by the storm, discovered by the daylight, and cut off by the revenue cutter, was making a desperate push for success in her hazard. And so all, watchers and watched, braced themselves for what might come about. Amongst the groups moved the tall figure of Mendoza, whispering and pointing, but keeping carefully hidden from the sight of the coastguards. He was evidently inciting them to some course from which they held back.

Closer and closer came the Sea Gull, lying down to the scuppers as she tacked; lightened as she was she made more leeway than was usual to so crank a boat. At last she got her head in the right direction for a run in, and, to the amazement of all who saw her, came full tilt into the outer basin, and, turning sharply round, ran into the inner basin under bare poles. There was not one present, smuggler or coastguard, who did not set down the daring attempt as simply suicidal. In a few seconds the boat stuck on the sandbank accumulated at the western end of the basin and stopped, her bows almost touching the side of the pier. The coastguards had not expected any such maneuver, and had taken their place on either side of the entrance to the inner basin, so that it took them a few seconds to run the length of the pier and come opposite the boat. The crowd of the smugglers and the smugglers' friends was so great that just as Neil and his brother began to shove out a plank from the bows to step ashore there was so thick a cluster round the spot that the lieutenant as he came could not see what was going on. Some little opposition was made to his passing through the mass of people, which was getting closer every instant, but his men closed up behind, and together they forced a way to the front before any one from the Sea Gull could spring on shore. A sort of angry murmur — that deep undertone which marks the passion of a mass — arose, and the lieutenant, recognizing its import, faced round like lightning, his revolver pointed straight in the faces of the crowd, whilst the men with him drew their cutlasses.

To Sailor Willy this appearance of action gave a relief from almost intolerable pain. He was in feverish anxiety about Maggie, but he could do nothing — nothing; and to an active and resolute man this feeling is in itself the worst of pain. His heart was simply breaking with suspense, and so it was that the sight of drawn weapons, in whatever cause, came like an anodyne to his tortured imagination. The flash of the cutlasses woke in him the instinct of action, and with a leaping heart he sprang down the narrow winding path that led to the quay.

Before the lieutenant's pistol the crowd fell back. It was not that they were afraid — for cowardice is pretty well unknown in Buchan — but authority, and especially in arms, has a special force with law-breakers. But the smugglers did not mean going back altogether now that their booty was so close to them, and the two bodies stood facing each other when Sailor Willy came upon the scene and stood beside the officers. Things were looking pretty serious when the resonant voice of MacWhirter was heard:

"What d'ye mean, men, crowdin' on the officers. Stand back, there, and let the coastguards come aboard an they will. There's naught here that they mayn't see."

The lieutenant turned and stepped on the plank — which Neil had by this time shoved on shore — and went on board, followed by two of his men, the other remaining with the boatman and Willy Barrow on the quay. Neil went straight to the officer, and said:

"I want to go ashore at once! Search me an ye will!" He spoke so rudely that the officer was angered, and said to one of the men beside him:

"Put your hands over him and let him go," adding, sotto voce, "He wants a lesson in manners!" The man lightly passed his hands over him to see that he had nothing contraband about him, and, being satisfied on the point, stood back and nodded to his officer, and Neil sprang ashore, and hurried off towards the village.

Willy had, by this time, a certain feeling of relief, for he had been thinking, and he knew that MacWhirter would not have been so ready to bring the coastguards on board if he had any contraband with him. Hope did for him what despair could not, for as he instinctively turned his eyes over the waste of angry sea, for an instant he did not know if it were the blood in his eyes or, in reality, the red of the dawn which had shot up over the eastern horizon.

Mendoza's men, having been carefully searched by one of the coastguards, came sullenly on shore and went to the back of the crowd, where their master, scowling and white-faced, began eagerly to talk with them in whispers. MacWhirter and his elder son busied themselves with apparent nonchalance in the needful matters of the landing, and the crowd seemed holding back for a spring. The suspense of all was broken by the incoming of a boat sent off from the revenue cutter, which, driven by four sturdy oarsmen, and steered by the commander himself, swept into the outer basin of the harbor, tossing amongst the broken waves. In the comparative shelter of the wall it turned, and driving into the inner basin pulled up on the slip beyond where the Sea Gull lay. The instant the boat touched, six bluejackets sprang ashore, followed by the commander, and all seven men marched quietly but resolutely to the quay opposite the Sea Gull's bow. The oarsmen followed, when they had hauled their boat up on the slip. The crowd now abandoned whatever had been its intention, and fell back looking and muttering thunder.

By this time the lieutenant was satisfied that the coble contained nothing that was contraband, and, telling its master so, stepped on shore just as Neil, with his face white as a sheet, and his eyes blazing, rushed back at full speed. He immediately attacked Sailor Willy:

"What hae ye dune wi' ma sister Maggie?"

He answered as quietly as he could, although there shot through his heart a new pain, a new anxiety:

"I know naught of her. I haven't seen her since last night, when Alice MacDonald was being married. Is she not at home?"

"Dinna ye ken damned weel that she's no'. Why did ye send her oot?" And he looked at him with the menace of murder in his eyes. The lieutenant saw from the looks of the two men that something was wrong, and asked Neil shortly:

78

"Where did you see her last?" Neil was going to make some angry reply, but in an instant Mendoza stepped forward, and in a loud voice gave instruction to one of his men who had been on board the Sea Gull to take charge of her, as she was his under a bill of sale. This gave Neil time to think, and his answer came sullenly:

"Nane o' ye're business — mind yer ain affairs!" MacWhirter, when he had seen Neil come running back, had realized the worst, and leaned on the taffrail of the boat, groaning. Mendoza's man sprang on board, and, taking him roughly by the shoulder, said:

"Come, clear out here. This boat is to Mendoza; get away!" The old man was so overcome with his feelings regarding Maggie that he made no reply, but quietly, with bent form, stepped on the plank and gained the quay. Willy Barrow rushed forward and took him by the hand and whispered to him:

"What does he mean?"

"He means," said the old man in a low, strained voice, "that for me an' him, an' to warn us she cam oot last nicht in the storm in a wee bit boat, an' that she is no' to her hame!" and he groaned. Willy was smitten with horror. This, then, was Maggie's high and desperate purpose when she left him. He knew now the meaning of those despairing words, and the darkness of the grave seemed to close over his soul. He moaned out to the old man: "She did not tell me she was going. I never knew it. O my God!" The old man, with the protective instinct of the old to the young, laid his hand on his shoulder, as he said to him in a broken voice:

"A ken it, lad! A ken it weel! She tell't me sae hersel! The sin is a' wi' me, though you, puir lad, must e'en bear yer share o' the pain!" The commander said quietly to the lieutenant:

"Looks queer, don't it — the coastguard and the smuggler whispering?"

"All right," came the answer, "I know Barrow; he is as true as steel, but he's engaged to the old man's daughter. But I gather there's something queer going on this morning about her. I'll find out. Barrow," he added, calling Willy to him, "what is it about MacWhirter's daughter?"

"I don't know for certain, sir, but I fear she was out at sea last night."

"At sea," broke in the commander; "at sea last night — how?"

"She was in a bit fishin'-boat," broke in MacWhirter. "Neighbors, hae ony o' ye seen her this mornin'? 'Twas ma son Andra's boat, that he keeps i' the Downans!" — another name for the Watter's Mou'. A sad silence that left the angry roar of the waves as they broke on the rocks and on the long strand in full possession was the only reply.

"Is the boat back in the Watter's Mou'?" asked the lieutenant sharply.

"No." said a fisherman. "A cam up jist noo past the Barley Mill, an' there's nae boat there."

"Then God help her, an' God forgie me," said MacWhirter, tearing off his cap and holding up his hands, "for A've killed her — her that sae loved her auld father, that she went oot alane in a bit boat i' the storm i' the nicht to save him frae the consequence o' his sin." Willy Barrow groaned, and the lieutenant turned to him: "Heart, man, heart! God won't let a brave girl like that be lost. That's the lass for a sailor's wife. 'Twill be all right — you'll be proud of her yet!"

But Sailor Willy only groaned despite the approval of his conscience; his words of last night came back to him. "Ye're no fit wife for me!" Now the commander spoke out to MacWhirter:

"When did you see her last?"

"Aboot twa o'clock i' the mornin'."

"Where?"

"Aboot twenty miles off the Scaurs."

"How did she come to leave you?"

"She pulled the boat that she cam in alongside the coble, an' got in by hersel — the last I saw o' her she had hoisted her sail an' was running nor'west . . . But A'll see her nae mair — a's ower wi' the puir, brave lass — an' wi' me, tae, that killed her — a's ower the noo — a's ower!" and he covered his face with his hands and sobbed. The commander said kindly enough, but with a stern gravity that there was no mistaking:

"Do I take it rightly that the girl went out in the storm to warn you?"

"Aye! Puir lass — 'twas an ill day that made me put sic a task on her — God forgie me!" and there and then he told them all of her gallant deed.

The commander turned to the lieutenant, and spoke in the quick, resolute, masterful accent of habitual command:

"I shall leave you the bluejackets to help — send your men all out, and scour every nook and inlet from Kirkton to Boddam. Out with all the lifeboats on the coast! And you, men!" he turned to the crowd, "turn out, all of you, to help! Show that there's some man's blood in you, to atone if you can for the wrong that sent this young girl out in a storm to save her father from you and your like!" Here he turned again to the lieutenant, "Keep a sharp eye on that man — Mendoza, and all his belongings. We'll attend to him later on: I'll be back before night."

"Where are you off to, Commander?"

"I'm going to scour the sea in the track of the storm where that gallant lass went last night. A brave girl that dared what she did for her father's sake is not to be lost without an effort; and, by God, she shan't lack it whilst I hold Her Majesty's command! Boatswain, signal the cutter full steam up — no, you! We mustn't lose time, and the boatswain comes with me. To your oars, men!"

The seamen gave a quick, sharp "Hurrah!" as they sprang to their places, whilst the man of the shore party to whom the order had been given climbed the sea-wall and telegraphed the needful orders; the crowd seemed to catch the enthusiasm of the moment, and scattered right and left to make search along the shore. In a few seconds the revenue boat was tossing on the waves outside the harbor, the men laying to their work as they drove her along, their bending oars keeping time to the swaying body of the commander, who had himself taken the tiller. The lieutenant said to Willy with thoughtful kindness:

"Where would you like to work on the search? Choose which part you will!" Willy instinctively touched his cap as he answered sadly:

"I should like to watch here, sir, if I may. She would make straight for the Watter's Mou'!"

*T*he search for the missing girl was begun vigorously, and carried on thoroughly and with untiring energy. The Port Erroll lifeboat was got out and proceeded up coast, and a telegram was sent to Kirkton to get out the lifeboat there, and follow up the shore to Port Erroll. From either place a body of men with ropes followed on shore keeping pace with the boat's progress. In the meantime the men of each village and hamlet all along the shore of Buchan from Kirkton to Boddam began a systematic exploration of all the openings on the coast. Of course there were some places where no search could at present be made. The Bullers, for instance, was well justifying its name with the wild turmoil of waters that fretted and churned between its rocky walls, and the neighborhood

of the Twa Een was like a seething caldron. At Dunbuy,
a great sheet of foam, perpetually renewed by the rush
and recoil of the waves among the rocks, lay like a great
white blanket over the inlet, and effectually hid any
flotsam or jetsam that might have been driven thither.
But on the high cliffs around these places, on every
coign of vantage, sat women and children, who kept
keen watch for aught that might develop. Every now
and again a shrill cry would bring a rush to the place
and eager eyes would follow the pointing hand of the
watcher who had seen some floating matter; but in
every case a few seconds and a little dispersing of the
shrouding foam put an end to expectation. Throughout that day the ardor of the searchers never abated.
Morning had come rosy and smiling over the waste of
heaving waters, and the sun rose and rose till its noon-
day rays beat down oppressively. But Willy Barrow
never ceased from his lonely vigil on the cliff. At
dinnertime a good-hearted woman brought him some
food, and in kindly sympathy sat by him in silence,
whilst he ate it. At first it seemed to him that to eat at
all was some sort of wrong to Maggie, and he felt that
to attempt it would choke him. But after a few mouth-
fuls the human need in him responded to the occasion,
and he realized how much he wanted food. The kindly
neighbor then tried to cheer him with a few words of
hope, and a many words of Maggie's worth, and left
him, if not cheered, at least sustained for what he had
to endure.

All day long his glass ranged the sea in endless,
ever-baffled hope. He saw the revenue boat strike away
at first towards Girdleness, and then turn and go out
to where Maggie had left the Sea Gull; and then under
full steam churn her way northwest through the fretted
seas. Now and again he saw boats, far and near, pass

on their way; and as they went through that wide belt of sea where Maggie's body might be drifting with the wreckage of her boat, his heart leaped and fell again under stress of hope and despair. The tide fell lower and ever lower, till the waves piling into the estuary roared among the rocks that paved the Watter's Mou'. Again and again he peered down from every rocky point in fear of seeing amid the turmoil — what, he feared to think. There was ever before his eyes the figure of the woman he loved, spread out rising and falling with the heaving waves, her long hair tossing wide and making an aureole round the upturned white face. Turn where he would, in sea or land, or in the white clouds of the summer sky, that image was ever before him, as though it had in some way burned into his iris.

Later in the afternoon, as he stood beside the crane, where he had met Maggie the night before, he saw Neil coming towards him, and instinctively moved from the place, for he felt that he would not like to meet on that spot, forever to be hallowed in his mind, Maggie's brother with hatred in his heart. So he moved slowly to meet him, and when he had got close to the flagstaff waited till he should come up, and swept once again the wide horizon with his glass — in vain. Neil, too, had begun to slow his steps as he drew nearer. Slower and slower he came, and at last stood close to the man whom in the morning he had spoken to with hatred and murder in his heart.

All the morning Neil had worked with a restless, feverish actively, which was the wonder of all. He had not stayed with the searching party with whom he had set out; their exhaustive method was too slow for him, and he soon distanced them, and alone scoured the whole coast as far as Murdoch Head. Then in almost complete despair, for his mind was satisfied that Maggie's body had never reached that part of the shore, he had retraced his steps almost at a run, and, skirting the sands of Cruden Bay, on whose wide expanse the beakers still rolled heavily and roared loudly, he glanced among the jagged rocks that lay around Whinnyfold and stretched under the water away to the Scaurs. Then he came back again, and the sense of desolation complete upon him moved his passionate heart to sympathy and pity. It is when the soul within us feels the narrow environments of our selfishness that she really begins to spread her wings.

Neil walked over the sand hills along Cruden Bay like a man in a dream. With a sailor's habit he watched the sea, and now and again had his attention attracted by the drifting masses of seaweed torn from its rocky bed by the storm. In such tossing black masses he sometimes thought Maggie's body might lie, but his instinct of the sea was too true to be long deceived. And then he began to take himself to task. Hitherto he had been too blindly passionate to be able to think of anything but his own trouble; but now, despite what he could do, the woe-stricken face of Sailor Willy would rise before his inner eye like the embodiment or the wraith of a troubled conscience. When once this train of argument had been started, the remorseless logic which is the mechanism of the spirit of conscience went on its way unerringly. Well he knew it was the ill-doing of which he had a share, and not the duty that Willy owed, that took his sister out alone on the stormy sea. He knew from her own lips that Willy had neither sent her nor even knew of her going, and the habit of fair play which belonged to his life began to exert an influence. The first sign of his change of mind was the tear that welled up in his eye and rolled down his cheek. "Poor Maggie! Poor Willy!" he murmured to himself, half unconsciously, "A'll gang to him an' tak it a' back!" With this impulse on him he quickened his steps, and never paused till he saw Willy Barrow before him, spyglass to eye, searching the sea for any sign of his lost love. Then his fears, and the awkwardness that a man feels at such a moment, no matter how poignant may be the grief that underlies it, began to trip him up. When he stood beside Willy Barrow, he said, with what bravery he could:

"I tak it a' back, Sailor Willy! Ye werena to blame! It was oor daein'! Will ye forgie me?" Willy turned and impulsively grasped the hand extended to him. In the midst of his overwhelming pain this was some little gleam of sunshine. He had himself just sufficient remorse to make the assurance of his innocence by another grateful. He knew well that if he had chosen to sacrifice his duty Maggie would never have gone out to sea, and though it did not even occur to him to repent of doing his duty, the mere temptation – the mere struggle against it, made a sort of foothold where flying remorse might for a moment rest. When the eyes of the two men met, Willy felt a new duty rise within his. He had always loved Neil, who was younger than himself, and was Maggie's brother, and he could not but see the look of anguish in the eyes that were so like Maggie's. He saw there something that in one way transcended his own pain, and made him glad that he had not on his soul the guilt of treachery to his duty. Not for the wide world would he have gazed into Maggie's eyes with such a look as that in his own. And yet – and yet – there came back to him with an overpowering flood of anguish the thought that, though the darkness had mercifully hidden it, Maggie's face, after she had tempted him, had had in it something of the same expression. It is a part of the penalty of being human that we cannot forbid the coming of thoughts, but it is a glory of humanity that we can wrestle with them and overcome them. Quick on the harrowing memory of Maggie's shame came the thought of Maggie's heroic self-devotion: her true spirit had found a way out of shame and difficulty, and the tribute of the lieutenant, "That's the lass for a sailor's wife!" seemed to ring in Willy's ears. As far as death was concerned, Willy Barrow did not fear it for himself, and how could he feel the fear for another. Such semblance of fear as had been in his distress was based on the selfishness that is a part of man's love, and in this wild hour of pain and distress became a thing of naught. All this reasoning, all this sequence of emotions, passed in a few seconds, and, as it seemed to him all at once, Willy Barrow broke out crying with the abandon which marks strong men when spiritual pain breaks down the barriers of their pride. Men of Willy's class seldom give way to their emotions. The prose of life is too continuous to allow of any habit of prolonged emotional indulgence; the pendulum swings back from fact to fact and things go on as before. So it was with Sailor Willy. His spasmodic grief was quick as well as fierce, like an April shower; and in a few seconds he had regained his calm. But the break, though but momentary, had relieved his pent-up feelings, and his heart beat more calmly for it. Then some of the love that he had for Maggie went out to her brother, and as he saw that the pain in his face did not lessen, a great pity overcame him and he tried to comfort Neil.

"Don't grieve, man. Don't grieve. I know well you'd give your heart's blood for Maggie" — he faltered as he spoke her name, but with a great gulp went on bravely: "There's your father — her father, we must try and comfort him. Maggie," here he lifted his cap reverently, "is with God! We, you and I, and all, must so bear ourselves that she shall not have died in vain." To Sailor Willy's tear-blurred eyes, as he looked upward, it seemed as if the great white gull which perched as he spoke on the yard of the flagstaff over his head was in some way an embodiment of the spirit of the lost girl, and, like the lightning phantasmagoria of a dream, there flitted across his mind many an old legend and eerie belief gained among the wolds and barrows of his Yorkshire home.

There was not much more to be said between the men, for they understood each other, and men of their class are not prone to speak more than is required. They walked northwards, and for a long time they stood together on the edge of the cliff, now and again gazing seawards, and ever and anon to where below their feet and falling tide was fretting and churning amongst the boulders at the entrance of the Watter's Mou'.

Neil was unconsciously watching his companion's face and following his thoughts, and presently said, as though in answer to something that had gone before: "Then ye think she'll drift in here, if onywhere?" Willy started as though he had been struck, for there seemed a positive brutality in the way of putting his own secret belief. He faced Neil quickly, but there was nothing in his face of any brutal thought. On the contrary, the lines of his face were so softened that all his likeness to his sister stood out so markedly as to make the heart of her lover ache with a fresh pang — a new sense, not of loss, but of what he had lost. Neil was surprised at the manner of his look, and his mind working back gave him the clue. All at once he broke out:

"O Willy mon, we'll never see her again! Never! never! till the sea gies up its dead; what can we dae, mon? what can we dae? what can we dae?"

Again there was a new wrench to Sailor Willy's heart. Here were almost Maggie's very words of the night before, spoken in the same despairing tone, in the same spot, and by one who was not only her well-beloved brother, but who was, as he stood in this abandonment of his grief, almost her living image. However, he did not know what to say, and he could do nothing but only bear in stolid patient misery the woes that came upon him. He did all that could be done — nothing — but stood in silent sympathy and waited for the storm in the remorseful young man's soul to pass. After a few minutes Neil recovered somewhat, and, pulling himself together, said to Willy with what bravery he could:

"A'll gang look after father. A've left him ower lang as't is!" The purpose of Maggie's death was beginning to bear fruit already.

He went across the field straight towards where his father's cottage stood under the brow of the slope towards the Water of Cruden. Sailor Willy watched him go with sadness, for anything that had been close to Maggie was dear to him, and Neil's presence had been in some degree an alleviation of his pain.

During the hours that followed he had one gleam of pleasure — something that moved him strangely in the midst of his pain. Early in the morning the news of Maggie's loss had been taken to the Castle, and all its household had turned out to aid vigorously in the search. In his talk with the lieutenant and his men, and from the frequent conversation of the villagers, the Earl had gathered pretty well the whole truth of what had occurred. Maggie had been a favorite with the ladies of the Castle, and it was as much on her account as his own that the Mastership of the Harbor had been settled prospectively on MacWhirter. That this arrangement was to be upset since the man had turned smuggler was taken for granted by all, and already rumor and surmise were busy in selecting a successor to the promise. The Earl listened but said nothing. Later on in the day, however, he strolled up the cliff where Willy paced on guard, and spoke with him. He had a sincere regard and liking for the fine young fellow, and when he saw his silent misery his heart went out to him. He tried to comfort him with hopes, but, finding that there was no response in Willy's mind, confined himself to praise of Maggie. Willy listened eagerly as he spoke of her devotion, her bravery, her noble spirit, that took her out on such a mission; and the words fell like drops of balm on the seared heart of her lover. But the bitterness of his loss was too much that he should be altogether patient, and he said presently:

"And all in vain! All in vain! she lost, and her father ruined, his character gone as well as all his means of livelihood — and all in vain! God might be juster than to let such a death as hers be in vain!"

"No, not in vain!" he answered solemnly, "such a deed as hers is never wrought in vain. God sees and hears, and His hand is strong and sure. Many a man in Buchan for many a year to come will lead an honester life for what she has done; and many a woman will try to learn her lesson in patience and self-devotion. God does not in vain put such thoughts into the minds of His people, or into their hearts the noble bravery to carry them out."

Sailor Willy groaned. "Don't think me ungrateful, my lord," he said, "for your kind words — but I'm half wild with trouble, and my heart is sore. Maybe it is as you say — and yet — and yet the poor lass went out to save her father and here he is, ruined in means, in character, in prospects — for who will employ him now just when he most wants it. Everything is gone — and she gone too that could have helped and comforted him!"

As he spoke there shot through the mind of his comforter a thought followed by a purpose not unworthy of that ancestor, whose heroism and self-devotion won an earldom with an ox-yoke as its crest, and the circuit of a hawk's flight as its dower. There was a new tone in the Earl's voice as he spoke:

"You mean about the harbor-mastership! Don't let that distress you, my poor lad. MacWhirter has lapsed a bit, but he has always borne an excellent character, and from all I hear he was sorely tempted. And, after all, he hasn't done — at least completed — any offence. Oh!" and here he spoke solemnly, "poor Maggie's warning did come in time. Her work was not in vain, though God help us all! she and those that loved her paid a heavy price for it. But even if MacWhirter had committed the offence, and it lay in my power, I should try to prove that her noble devotion was not without its purpose — or its reward. It is true that I might not altogether trust MacWhirter until, at least, such time as by good service he had re-established his character. But I would and shall trust the father of Maggie MacWhirter, that gave her life for him; and well I know that there isn't an honest man or woman in Buchan that won't say the same. He shall be the harbormaster if he will. We shall find in time that he has reared again the love and respect of all men. That will be Maggie's monument; and a noble one too in the eyes of God and of men!"

He grasped Willy's hand in his own strong one, and the hearts of both men, the gentle and the simple, went out each to the other, and became bound together as men's hearts do when touched with flame of any kind.

When he was alone Willy felt somehow more easy in his mind. The bitterest spirit of all is woe — the futility of Maggie's sacrifice — was gone, exorcised by the hopeful words and kind act of the Earl, and the resilience of his manhood began to act.

And now there came another distraction to his thoughts — an ominous weather change. It had grown colder as the day went on, but now the heat began to be oppressive, and there was a deadly stillness in the air; it was manifest that another storm was at hand. The sacrifice of the night had not fully appeased the storm-gods. Somewhere up in that Northern Unknown, where the Fates weave their web of destiny, a tempest was brewing which would soon boil over. Darker and darker grew the sky, and more still and silent and oppressive grew the air, till the cry of a sea bird or the beating of the waves upon the rocks came as distinct and separate things, as though having no counterpart in the active world. Towards sunset the very electricity in the air made all animate nature so nervous that men and women could not sit quiet, but moved restlessly. Susceptible women longed to scream out and vent their feelings, as did the cattle in the meadows with their clamorous lowing, or the birds wheeling restlessly aloft with articulate cries. Willy Barrow stuck steadfastly to his post. He had some feeling — some presentiment that there would soon be a happening — what, he knew not; but, as all his thoughts were of Maggie, it must surely be of her. It might have been that the thunderous disturbance wrought on a system overtaxed almost beyond human endurance, for it was two whole nights since he had slept. Or it may have been that the recoil from despair was acting on his strong nature in the way that drives men at times to desperate deeds, when they rush into

The Watter's Mou'

the thick of battle, and, fighting, die. Or it may simply have been that the seaman in him spoke through all the ways and offices of instinct and habit, and that with the foreknowledge of coming stress woke the power that was to combat with it. For great natures of the fighting kind move with their surroundings, and the spirit of the sailor grew with the storm pressure whose might he should have to brave.

Down came the storm in one wild, frenzied burst. All at once the waters seemed to rise, throwing great sheets of foam from the summit of the lifting waves. The wind whistled high and low, and screamed as it swept through the rigging of the flagstaff. Flashes of lightning and rolling thunderclaps seemed to come together, so swift their succession. The rain fell in torrents, so that within a few moments the whole earth seemed one filmy sheet, shining in the lightning flashes that rent the black clouds, and burn and rill and runlet roared with rushing water. All through the hamlet men and women, even the hardiest, fled to shelter — all save the one who paced the rocks above the Watter's Mou', peering as he had done for many an hour down into the depths below him in the pauses of his seaward glance. Something seemed to tell him that Maggie was coming closer to him. He could feel her presence in the air and the sea; and the memory of that long, passionate kiss, which had made her his, came back, not as a vivid recollection, but as something of the living present. To and fro he paced between the flagstaff and the edge of the rocks; but each turn he kept further and further from the flagstaff, as though some fatal fascination was holding him to the Watter's Mou'. He saw the great waves come into the cove tumbling and roaring; dipping deep under the lee of the Ship's Starn in wide patches of black, which in the dark silence of their onward sweep stood out in strong contrast to the white turmoil of the churning waters under his feet. Every now and again a wave greater than all its fellows — what fishermen call the "sailor's wave" — would ride in with all the majesty of resistless power, shutting out for a moment the jagged whiteness of the submerged rocks, and sweeping up the cove as though the bringer of some royal message from the sea.

As one of these great waves rushed in, Willy's heart beat loudly, and for a second he looked around as though for some voice, from whence he knew not, which was calling to him. Then he looked down and saw, far below him, tossed high upon the summit of the wave, a mass that in the gloom of the evening and the storm looker like a tangle of wreckage — spar and sail and rope — twirling in the rushing water round a dead woman, whose white face was set in an aureole of floating hair. Without a word, but with the bound of a panther, Willy Barrow sprang out on the projecting point of rock, and plunged down into the rushing wave whence he could meet that precious wreckage and grasp it tight.

*D*own in the village the men were talking in groups as the chance of the storm had driven them to shelter. In the rocket-house opposite the Salmon Fisher's store had gathered a big cluster, and they were talking eagerly of all that had gone by. Presently one of them said:

"Men, oughtn't some o' us to gang abeen the rocks and bide a wee wi' Sailor Willy? The puir lad is nigh daft wi' his loss, an 'a wee bit companionship wouldna be bad for him." To which a sturdy youth answered as he stepped out:

"A'l go bide wi' him. It must be main lonely for him in the guardhouse the nicht. An' when he's relieved, as A hear he is to be, by Michael Watson ower frae Whinnyfold, A'll gang wi' him or tak him hame wi' me. Mither'll be recht glad to thole for him!" and drawing his oilskin closer round his neck he went out in the storm. As he walked up the path to the cliff the storm seemed to fade away — the clouds broke, and through the wet mist came gleams of fading twilight; and when he looked eastwards from the cliff the angry sea was all that was of storm, for in the sky was every promise of fine weather to come. He went straight to the guardhouse and tried to open the door, but it was locked; then he went to the side and looked in. There was just sufficient light to see that the place was empty. So he went along the cliff looking for Willy. It was now light enough to see all round, for the blackness of the sky overhead had passed, the heavy clouds being swept away by the driving wind; but nowhere could he see any trace of the man he sought. He went all along the cliff up the Watter's Mou', till, following the downward trend of the rock, and splashing a way through the marsh — now like a quagmire, so saturated was it with the heavy rainfall — he came to the shallows opposite the Barley Mill. Here he met a man from The Bullers, who had come along by the Castle, and him he asked if he had seen Willy Barrow on his way. The decidedly negative answer "A've seen nane. It's nae a night for ony to be oot than can bide wi'in!" made him think that all might not be well with Sailor Willy, and so he went back again on his search, peering into every hole and cranny as he went. At the flagstaff he met some of his companions, who, since the storm had passed, had come to look for weather signs and to see what the sudden tempest might have brought about. When they heard that there was no sign of the coastguard they separated, searching for him, and shouting lest he might have fallen anywhere and hear their voices.

All that night they searched, for each minute made it more apparent that all was not well with him; but they found no sign. The waves still beat into the Watter's Mou' with violence, for though the storm had passed the sea was a wide-stretching mass of angry waters, and curling white crowned every wave. But with the outgoing tide the rocky bed of the cove broke up the waves, and they roared sullenly as they washed up the estuary.

In the grey of the morning a fisher-boy rushed up to a knot of men who were clustered round the guard-house and called to them:

"There's somethin' wollopin' aboot i' the shallows be the Barley Mill! Come an' get it oot! It looks like some ane!" So there was a rush made to the place. When they got to the islands of sea-grass the ebbing tide had done its work, and stranded the "something" which had rolled amid the shallows.

There, on the very spot whence the boat had set sail on its warning errand, lay its wreckage, and tangled in it the body of the noble girl who had steered it — her brown hair floating wide and twined round the neck of Sailor Willy, who held her tight in his dead arms.

The requiem of the twain was the roar of the breaking waves and the screams of the white birds that circled round the Watter's Mou'.